FAVOURITE CAROLS

for Flute

FAVOURITE CAROLS

for Flute

kevin
mayhew

We hope you enjoy *Favourite Carols for Flute*.
Further copies of this and our many other books are available
from your local Kevin Mayhew stockist.

In case of difficulty, or to request a catalogue,
please contact the publisher direct by writing to:

The Sales Department
KEVIN MAYHEW LTD
Buxhall
Stowmarket
Suffolk IP14 3BW

Phone 01449 737978
Fax 01449 737834
E-mail info@kevinmayhewltd.com

First published in Great Britain in 2002 by Kevin Mayhew Ltd.

© Copyright 2002 Kevin Mayhew Ltd.

ISBN 1 84003 981 7
ISMN M 57024 133 0
Catalogue No: 3611713

0 1 2 3 4 5 6 7 8 9

Cover design: Angela Selfe
Music setter: Donald Thomson
Proof reader: Tracy Cook

Printed and bound in Great Britain

Contents

Angels from the realms of glory

French or Flemish melody

2 verses

Refrain

Away in a manger

William James Kirkpatrick (1838-1921)

2 verses

Christians, awake!

John Wainwright (1723-1768)

2 verses

Good King Wenceslas

From *Piae Cantiones* (1582)

2 verses

Hark, the herald-angels sing

Adapted from Felix Mendelssohn (1809-1847)
by William Hayman Cummings (1831-1915)

2 verses

I saw three ships

Traditional English melody

3 verses

In the bleak midwinter

Gustav Holst (1874-1934)

2 verses

O come, all ye faithful

Attributed to John Francis Wade (1711-1786)

2 verses

Refrain

O little town of Bethlehem

Traditional English melody

2 verses

Once in royal David's city

Henry John Gauntlett (1805-1876)

2 verses

See, amid the winter's snow

John Goss (1800-1880)

2 verses

Silent night

Franz Grüber (1787-1863)

2 verses

The angel Gabriel from heaven came

Traditional Basque melody

2 verses

The first Nowell

Traditional English melody

2 verses

Refrain

While shepherds watched

From Thomas Este's *Psalter* (1592)

3 verses